I Told You I Can PLAY!

By Brian Jordan

Illustrations by Cornelius Van Wright and Ying-Hwa Hu

MARIMBA BOOKS
An imprint of Kensington Publishing Corp. and Hudson Publishing Group LLC
850 Third Avenue, New York, NY 10022

Previously published in hardcover under the Just Us Books imprint.

All Kensington titles, imprints, and distributed lines are available at special quantity discounts for bulk purchases for sales promotions, premiums, fund-raising, and educational or institutional use.

Special book excerpts or customized printings can also be created to fit specific needs.
For details, write or phone the office of the Kensington special sales manager:
Kensington Publishing Corp., 850 Third Avenue, New York, NY 10022, attn: Special Sales Department, 1-800-221-2647.

MARIMBA BOOKS and the Marimba Books logo are trademarks of Kensington Publishing Corp. and Hudson Publishing Group LLC.

ISBN-13: 978-1-60349-001-6   ISBN-10: 1-60349-001-9

First Marimba Books printing: September 2008

10 9 8 7 6 5 4 3 2 1

Printed in the United States of America

D1410593

When Brian was a little boy,
he was eager to do everything.

But he especially loved to play sports.

Brian **loved**
to play basketball.

He **loved** to play baseball.

And he **loved**
to play football.

Brian's twin brother and sister were two and a half years older than he was.

Brian wanted to do everything they did.

He was determined to keep up with them.

But the twins didn't like their little brother following them around.

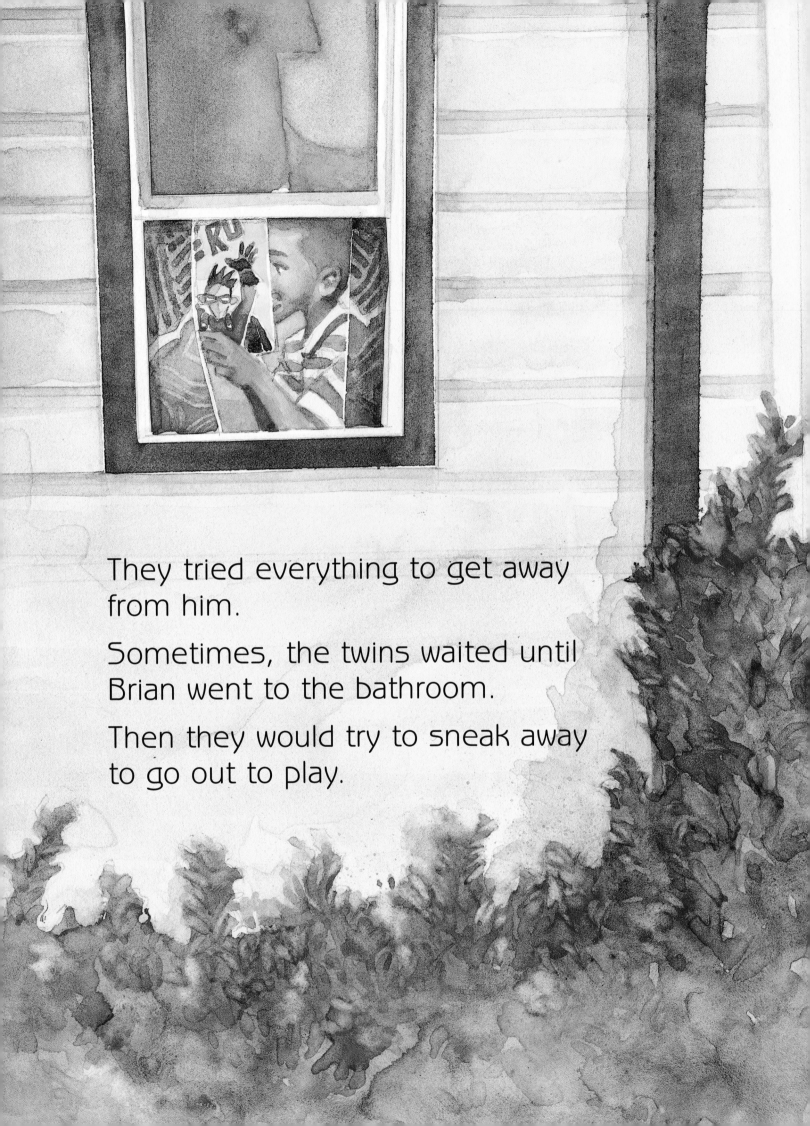

They tried everything to get away
from him.

Sometimes, the twins waited until
Brian went to the bathroom.

Then they would try to sneak away
to go out to play.

But their Mom and Dad always spoiled the plan.

When Brian was a little older, he wanted to play with his brother and his brother's friends.

But Brian's brother thought a six-year-old was too young to hang out with nine-year-olds.

Besides, he was the only one who had to babysit a little brother.

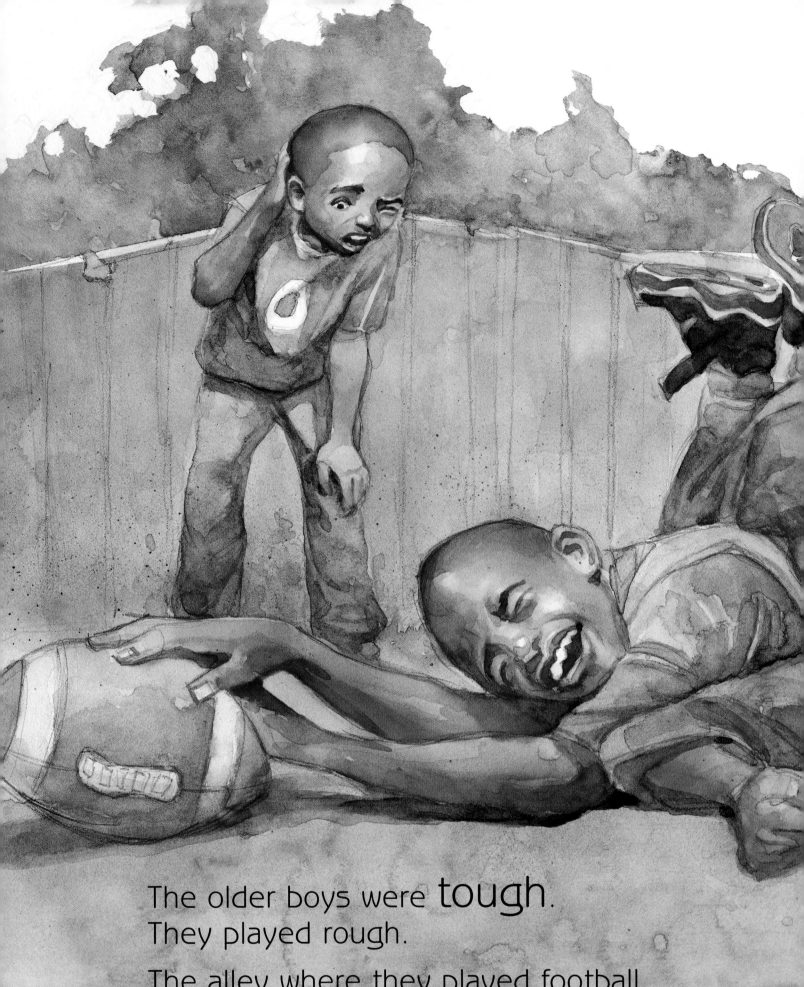

The older boys were tough.
They played rough.

The alley where they played football
was as hard as a rock.

But they would crash to the hard field,
bounce back up and keep playing.

So Brian knew he had to be tough, too.

Brian wanted to play with them
but they wouldn't let him.
"You're too little!"
his brother said.

"But I can play,"
Brian insisted.

One day Brian overheard his brother talking to a friend on the telephone.

They were planning to play a game.

"I want to play, too,"
Brian said.

"I told you, you're too little.
You'll get hurt," said his brother.

Brian was so disappointed.

He had to watch his brother and his brother's friends play football.

They were having so much fun.

Suddenly, a player's mother called.

"Johnnie, come home **now!**"
she demanded.

Now another player was needed
to replace Johnnie.

Brian jumped to his feet.
"I can play. Let me play!"
he pleaded.

Brian's brother thought for a moment.

"Alright, come on," he said.

Maybe Brian will learn a lesson. He'll see that he's too little to play with us, Brian's brother said to himself.

Brian was so **excited**. Finally, he could show everyone that he could play.

At first, Brian's teammates didn't give him a chance. How could he show them he could play if they wouldn't let him run with the ball?

Then, just as his brother was being tackled, he tossed the ball to Brian.

Brian caught it.

Brian ran with the ball.

One boy tried to tackle Brian,
but Brian dodged him.

He dodged another boy and then another.

Kids standing on the sidelines cheered as
Brian raced up the field.

"Go Brian!
Go Brian!" they yelled.

Then a much bigger player caught Brian.
"Thud!" He threw Brian to the hard ground.
Brian lay there. His eyes began to tear.

"Touchdown!" someone yelled.
"Brian scored a touchdown!"

All the players gathered around the new star.

Some patted him on the back.

Brian had done something really special for a six-year-old.

He had scored a touchdown against his brother's tough friends.

"That was great!" a tall boy said.

Brian looked at his older brother. He held the football firmly in his hands and said,

"I told you I can play!"

BRIAN JORDAN FOUNDATION

"We're dedicated to helping kids succeed in life by helping them to stay focused,
dedicated and determined."

Brian Jordan believes that every child has the potential for excellence. That is one of the reasons he created the Brian Jordan Foundation (www.brianjordanfoundation.com) in 1998. The foundation is dedicated to helping children build healthy minds and strong bodies and to creating supportive places where children can learn and grow. It serves its mission by focusing on education and facilities, advocacy, health and wellness, and research. The foundation also offers college scholarships to deserving students.

This book is dedicated to my children: Kenley, Briana, Kaleb and Bryson
—Love Daddy, B. O. J.

For Christopher
—C.V.W & Y-H.H.